THE WOODEN DOLL

THE WOODEN DOLL

SUSAN BONNERS

LOTHROP, LEE & SHEPARD BOOKS ~ NEW YORK

Many years ago, I went to visit my grandma and grandpa. I was excited. For the first time, I was staying with them by myself. Grandma put her feather comforter on the floor for me to sleep on. I snuggled down into it.

"Good night, Stefcha," she said, turning out the light.

Grandma was the only one who ever called me by that name. To everybody else, I was Stephanie, except Grandpa. He always called me Stephania.

"Grandma, could you put on a night-light?"

"We don't have one, Stefcha." She leaned down and patted my head. "You just close your eyes. Next thing you know, birds are singing. Maybe tomorrow Grandpa can take you for a walk down to the river."

Grandma went into the bedroom, clicking the door shut behind her. I tried to hear what she and Grandpa were saying to each other. I didn't think they were talking English.

In the dark, the house felt strange and a little scary. I closed my eyes and thought of the times Grandpa and I had sat together on the riverbank, not talking, just watching.

Suddenly Grandpa would point. "See there? Turtle is climbing on that log."

Then he would skip stones across the water for me— three, four, five skips in a row.

But morning was hours away.

The light in the bedroom went out. The house was silent, except for Grandma's old clock. Tick. Tick. Tick. Tick. The clock began chiming. Bong. Bong. Bong. I ducked my head under the covers. When the chiming stopped, I peeked out.

Next to the clock stood a beautiful wooden doll. Grandma had told me that it belonged to Grandpa. He had brought it with him from Poland, a long time ago. If something happened to it, he could never get another.

It wasn't like any doll I'd ever seen before. The hands and face, even the clothes, were painted on. I wanted to play with the doll, but Grandma had always told me, "Not yet. When you're older, ask Grandpa." Maybe this visit I was old enough.

When I woke up, the bedroom door was open and the bed was made. In the kitchen, the big soup kettle on the stove rattled its lid. I was afraid Grandma and Grandpa had gone somewhere. Then I heard Grandma's footsteps in the basement.

As I went down the steps, I heard Grandma humming to herself. When she saw me, she smiled.

"Come. Let Grandma fix pigtails for you." She pulled two rubber bands out of her apron pocket. "Oh," she said, combing back my hair with her fingers, "look who's under here!"

"I can help with the wash, Grandma." I began picking up armfuls of clothes from the laundry basket and handing them to her. "Grandma, can I have the doll that's on top of the cabinet? Just for a little while?"

"You know that's Grandpa's, sweetheart. Grandma can't give you that."

"Maybe he wouldn't mind. You could ask him, Grandma."

"Why don't you ask him, Stefcha? Talk to him. He likes that."

I wasn't so sure. Lots of times when I talked to Grandpa he seemed to be thinking of something else.

I sat down at the grindstone where Grandpa sharpened his tools and pumped the treadle. The big stone began to spin. I remembered how Grandpa had sharpened his pocket knife on it last summer before he fixed my kite. Grandpa knew how to fix everything.

Just then, I heard him above us, filling the watering can from the pump.

"Grandpa, I can do that!" I ran up the stairs and out the back door.

Grandpa was bent over, pumping the handle hard and fast. I put my hands on top of his and pumped with him. When the can was full, Grandpa stood up and opened the top button on his flannel shirt. His skin was brown from the sun. I thought he looked like an Indian chief.

I wanted to carry the can to the garden, but Grandpa motioned me away and took the handle himself. Then he took my hand.

Against my fingertips, his palm felt like sandpaper. My thumb slipped into the place where he had no middle finger. Grandma had told me he'd lost it in an accident at work, a long time ago. I wondered if it had hurt a lot and how it felt to have no middle finger. Did he ever think about it anymore?

We began to water the garden—up one row, down the next. Bees buzzed all around us, but Grandpa didn't seem to mind, so I wasn't afraid. The sunlight made little diamonds where the water droplets bounced on the leaves.

At the end of a row, Grandpa stooped down and picked something out of the dirt. He dropped it into my hand.

"That's a worm, Grandpa!"

"Yah. We put him back. Good for plants."

"How do you know that, Grandpa?" He didn't answer. I didn't know if he'd heard me.

We watered another row in silence. I wanted to ask Grandpa about the doll, but he seemed to have forgotten that I was there.

Finally I said, "Let me hold the can myself, Grandpa."

"Too heavy for you," Grandpa said, but I kept asking. "Okay, okay," he said at last. "Like this. Back and forth."

I tried to sway the can the way he did, but it was still heavy and the water inside kept sloshing. I struggled to hold it steady. Grandpa shook his head.

"Too much, too much one place. You make flood." He put his hand over mine and guided the can.

"I can do it, Grandpa." But he wasn't listening. He kept his hand over mine. I didn't know how to tell him that I didn't want him to hold the can for me. I wanted to show him how strong I was. I could really help him.

"Look at that." Grandpa clicked his tongue. "You got water all over yourself."

"I'm fine, Grandpa."

"No, no. Better let Grandpa do this."

It was no use. I let go of the can and let Grandpa finish the last row himself. Suddenly I didn't want to help anymore. Grandpa turned and started toward the shed.

"Grandpa," I said quickly, "can I have the doll on Grandma's cabinet? Just for a little while?"

Grandpa stopped. At first he looked puzzled. Then he said, "Oh, no, Stephania, not that doll. She's not for playing. She's old. She could break if you drop her."

"I wouldn't, Grandpa."

"No, Stephania." His voice was stern. "She's not a toy." He shook the last drops out of the watering can and turned away.

At lunch, Grandpa just looked down into his soup bowl and ate. As soon as he was finished, he put down his spoon, pushed back his chair, and went into the living room. I heard the sofa springs creak as he lay down.

I carried the dishes to Grandma at the sink.

"Grandma, is Grandpa mad at me?"

Grandma looked surprised. "No, why, Stefcha?"

"He didn't say anything at lunch. Maybe he thinks I bother him."

Grandma patted my shoulder. "You know, Grandpa never says too much, not even to Grandma."

"He didn't want me to help him in the garden. He doesn't think I can do it right."

"Grandpa's just tired, sweetheart. Up early, working all morning." She put down her dishcloth. "You play by yourself now. Nice quiet game." She went to the bedroom for her nap.

Grandma didn't understand what I meant. Grandpa would never let me have the doll. He'd be afraid I'd drop it. If only I were tall, like Grandma, I could take the doll down myself and put it back before anyone woke up. Taking the doll down for a minute couldn't hurt. I only wanted to look at it.

Then I had an idea.

I slipped out of my shoes and tiptoed into the dining room. A floorboard creaked. I froze, listening to Grandpa's steady breathing. Quietly I dragged the nearest chair over the rug to the cabinet, climbed on the seat, and reached up.

The doll was much heavier than I thought it would be. As I tipped it forward, something inside rattled softly. For a second, I was sure the doll was going to crash behind me to the floor. Holding my breath, I backed off the chair.

My stomach fluttered as I closed the kitchen door
and sat down at the table. As I ran my fingers over the
smooth paint, my thumb hit a crack, all around the
doll's waist. I twisted the lower part, holding the head
tight. All at once, the doll popped open.

Another doll stood inside.

This one was a man. I saw the crack around his
waist. I eased off the top. I knew it—another doll.
This one was a girl.

I began to make a line of dolls. One, two, three, four. Mother, father, sister, brother. Five, six, seven. The dolls got smaller and smaller. Eight, nine. I got to the edge of the table. Ten. That one was the size of a peanut. I pulled, but it was empty. I put the two halves together and counted the dolls again. Ten.

Each doll was different. I picked up my favorite, the largest one, and turned it over to see if the bottom was painted, too. It wasn't, but letters were carved into it.

I turned them to the light. I saw my own name, the name Grandpa always called me, *Stephania*.

The kitchen door swung open. Grandma stood in the doorway.

"Stefcha!"

"I was going to put them back, Grandma. Grandma, look. My name is on the bottom. Did Grandpa put it there? Is the doll for me?"

Grandma shook her finger at me, but then she sat down at the table and took one of the dolls in her hand. For a minute, she seemed far away. Then she turned to me.

"You ask Grandpa. Tell him you took his doll down. Then you ask him about your name." I thought Grandma was hiding a smile.

"Please, Grandma."

"No. You ask Grandpa." She began putting the dolls inside one another again.

I was confused. If Grandpa knew he was going to give me the doll, why hadn't he told me before? Would he be very angry that I took it down myself? As I watched Grandma put the doll back on top of the cabinet, I tried to think of what to say to him.

⁓ ⁓ ⁓

After dinner, Grandma sat in her armchair and began crocheting a new square for the tablecloth she was making. I sat on the sofa and pretended to read the newspaper with Grandpa.

Finally I said, "Grandpa, I looked at your doll this afternoon. Just for a minute."

"Uh-hmm. Yah, when you're bigger." He turned another page. Then he looked at Grandma. "What she talk about?"

"I took the doll down, Grandpa," I said quietly. "I climbed on the chair."

"Stephania! You could hurt yourself! Why you do that?"

"I didn't hurt myself, Grandpa. I just wanted to see it."

"Can you beat that?" he said to Grandma. He let the paper crumple in his lap. He didn't seem angry, just surprised.

"Grandpa," I said after a minute, "I saw what you put on the bottom of the doll."

"I put something on the bottom?"

"My name, Grandpa. I saw it."

He didn't seem to understand. Then, all of a sudden, he said, "Oh. I see. I see." He watched Grandma crochet a few more loops on her square. "Okay," he said at last. He patted my foot. "Grandpa explain to you."

He pushed himself off the sofa and got the wooden doll. Then he sat down and put his arm around me.

"You know why your name is Stephania?"

I looked at him. I'd never thought about it.

"You got my mother's name. She was Stephania, too. That's my mother's name here. This belonged to her. My father gave her this when I was born. He put her name there. Long time ago."

All afternoon, I'd thought Grandpa would tell me that the doll was meant for me someday. Now I understood. It wasn't for me at all. I slid away from his arm.

Grandpa looked at Grandma, then back at me. "Just think." He shook my shoulder. "One time your poor old grandpa was a tiny little baby. Got lost in the covers lots of times."

I knew Grandpa was trying to make me laugh, but I was too disappointed. Besides, I couldn't think of Grandpa being a baby. I had seen him carry long wooden ladders and heavy water buckets, two at a time.

Grandpa turned the doll right side up and looked it over.

"My father told me he saved and saved to buy this. Mother so surprised. She couldn't believe farmer could afford nice doll like this."

"You were born on a farm?" So that's how Grandpa knew about earthworms. I wished I had been born on a farm. "Did you have a horse to ride? And a barn with cows?"

Grandpa looked at Grandma. "Stephania think we have big farm like she see here." They nodded to each other.

"Not really a farm, Stefcha. Just a few fields, not even close to the house," Grandma said. "Grandpa's family didn't have so much. One small house, divided in the middle. Animals on one side, family on the other."

Grandpa laughed. "Just one old horse for plowing, not for rides. A cow. A few chickens. My mother sold eggs to get money for shoes and such. No money to buy a lot of animals."

Grandpa was quiet for a minute.

"I had two brothers, much older than me. I hardly knew them. They worked in the fields with mother and father all day. Then I worked, too, when I got big enough. Not even as big as you." Grandpa took a deep breath. "Lots of work there. Work every day till dark."

Grandpa brushed his hand over my head. "You know, Marisha, my mother had hair about this color, maybe little darker. She didn't want me to leave Poland, but I was stubborn, just like our Stephania here. She gave me this doll the day I left. Told me, 'Take care of yourself.' I didn't know then I'd never see her again. I was just a boy, only seventeen."

"Did she die?"

"Yes, Stephania. Long time ago."

For a while, I didn't say anything. I was thinking about a little boy, sitting all alone by the window while it got darker and darker. He was wondering when his parents and his brothers would come home. No wonder Grandpa was so quiet. He never had anybody to talk to when he was little. I was glad he had me and Grandma to talk to when he wanted, even though that wasn't very often.

I looked up at Grandpa. I thought he looked sad. I didn't want him to be. I tried to think of something to say. All I could think of was a woman in a long red skirt and a blue babushka waving good-bye. A tall boy was walking away through a field, carrying the doll under his arm.

Then I had an idea. I held up the doll. "I bet your mother looked just like this, didn't she, Grandpa?"

He laughed. "Yes, Stephania, just like this. Dark eyes and brown hair and a babushka."

Grandpa picked me up and put me in his lap. "I tell you what, Stephania. You're a pretty big girl now. You think you could take care of Grandpa's doll if I give her to you?"

"Grandpa! You mean it's mine?"

"Sure. Look." He tipped the doll over. "That's your name there!"

I was so happy, I couldn't say anything.

"Why don't we keep her for you, Stefcha?" said Grandma. "Then you would have a doll here when you visit."

I looked up at Grandpa. Maybe he would miss the doll if I took her away.

"But I could have her when I wanted, couldn't I, Grandpa?"

Grandpa stood up with me in his arms. "You want to see her, you just ask Grandpa."

He carried me over to the cabinet and lifted me up.
Very gently, I set the doll down.
 "Grandpa, I'll take good care of her, I promise!"
And I have, to this very day.

To my grandparents—
and to all those who left one world behind
to make their way in another.

First Edition   1   2   3   4   5   6   7   8   9   10

Library of Congress Cataloging in Publication Data
Bonners, Susan. The wooden doll / by Susan Bonners.
p.   cm. Summary: Visiting her grandparents' house, Stephanie learns the origin of Grandpa's beautiful wooden doll.
ISBN 0-688-08280-7 —ISBN 0-688-08282-3 (lib. bdg.)   [1. Dolls—Fiction. 2. Grandparents—Fiction.]   I. Title.
PZ7.B64253Wo   1991   [E]—dc20
90-33647   CIP   AC

DUE DATE

FEB. 1 7 1992			
OCT. 1 6 1994			
JAN 0 2 97			
JAN 2 9 97			
OCT 1 7 98			
			Printed in USA